To my double agents:
Caroline Walsh and Rebecca Watson – K.G.

To Lucy Napper – N.S.

Read about more Daisy adventures in **EAT YOUR PEAS**,
winner of the Children's Book Award, **YOU DO!**,
REALLY, REALLY, YUK! and **A BUNCH OF DAISIES**

006 AND A BIT
A BODLEY HEAD BOOK 978 0 370 32876 8 (from January 2007)
0 370 32876 0

First published in Great Britain in 2006 by The Bodley Head,
an imprint of Random House Children's Books

1 3 5 7 9 10 8 6 4 2

Set in Lemonade

RANDOM HOUSE CHILDREN'S BOOKS
61–63 Uxbridge Road, London W5 5SA
A division of The Random House Group Ltd

RANDOM HOUSE AUSTRALIA (PTY) LTD
20 Alfred Street, Milsons Point, Sydney,
New South Wales 2061, Australia

RANDOM HOUSE NEW ZEALAND LTD
18 Poland Road, Glenfield, Auckland 10, New Zealand

RANDOM HOUSE (PTY) LTD
Isle of Houghton, Corner Boundary Road & Carse O'Gowrie,
Houghton 2198, South Africa

THE RANDOM HOUSE GROUP Limited Reg. No. 954009

www.kidsatrandomhouse.co.uk/daisy

A CIP catalogue record for this book is available from the British Library.

Printed and bound in Singapore

006 and a Bit

Kes Gray & Nick Sharratt

THE BODLEY HEAD
LONDON

Daisy had made up her mind. She wasn't going to be a girl any more. She was going to be a spy.

She had drawn a spy's moustache on her top lip with a black felt-tip pen.

She had found some dark glasses in a drawer.

She had found some secret spy gadgets in her mum's bedroom. All she had to do now was speak in code.

(Code is a special spy language that only spies understand. Daisy had seen it used in spy films; now this time it was for real.)

Daisy frowned mysteriously and crept unseen into the kitchen.

"Hello, Daisy," said Mum. "What do you want for tea tonight?"

"The ostriches will be swimming in tomato sauce this evening," said Daisy.

(which, as any spy knows, means "a big portion of chicken nuggets and lots of ketchup, please!")

Daisy's *mum* stared at Daisy and scratched her head.

"Why are you speaking in silly words?" asked Daisy's *mum*.

"They're not silly words," whispered Daisy mysteriously.

"It's secret spy language. And *my* name isn't Daisy any more. It's 006 and a Bit."

"And what are you intending to do with *my* hairbrush, 006 and a Bit?" asked Daisy's *mum*.

"It's not a hairbrush. It's *my* secret spy telephone," said Daisy.

"And where are *you* going with *my* perfume bottle?" asked Daisy's *mum.*

"It's not your perfume bottle," said Daisy.
"It's *my* invisible ink."

"And would I be wrong in thinking that is *my* hairdryer?" said Daisy's *mum.*

"Yes," whispered Daisy. "It's not a hairdryer.

It's *my* secret baddie zapper."

Daisy's *mum* shook her head and went to find the ironing board.

006 and a Bit slipped invisibly into the back garden.

"Hello, Daisy," said her neighbour, "how are you today?"

"Good afternoon, Agent Goldfish," said Daisy.

"Are your fins green or purple today?"

(which, as any spy knows, means

"I'm fine thanks, Mrs Pike,

how are you?")

Mrs Pike stared strangely at Daisy and
went to mow her grass.

Daisy slipped invisibly across the garden and went to give an important message to Mrs Pike's cat.
"Meet me by the Golden Palace," she whispered,
"and bring your furry overcoat."
(which, as any spy knows, means, "Hello, Tiptoes, why don't you come and sit by the shed? I want to stroke you.")

Tiptoes took one look at Daisy's hairdryer
and skedaddled over the wall.

Daisy dabbed on some more invisible ink and peeped
out of the garden gate. "No one will be able
to see me now," she smiled.

"Hello, Daisy," said her best friend Gabby.

"Can you come out to play?"

"The laundry basket is full and the big busy beaver
has many clothes to fold," Daisy said.

(which, as any spy knows, means, "Hi Gabby! I'll just
ask my mum. She's doing the ironing.")

But Gabby gave Daisy a very strange look and
went to find someone else to play with.

Daisy took off her glasses and walked miserably back indoors.
"What's the matter, 006 and a Bit?" asked her *mum*.
"Aren't you playing spies any more?"
"No I'm not," sighed Daisy. "No one understands my
spy language. They just look at me as though I'm silly."

Daisy's *mum* stopped ironing
and put her arm around
Daisy's shoulders.
"That must be because
they're not real spies,"
whispered her *mum*.
"If they were, they would
understand everything
you are saying."

Daisy trudged into the living room and slumped onto the sofa. "Well they don't understand what I'm saying. There aren't any real spies around here, no one understands me and I'm not being a spy any more. Being a spy is stupid," she grumbled.

Daisy was just about to turn on the TV,
when a mysterious-looking stranger with
a purple moustache and beard poked his
head around the door. He had dark
glasses on, just like Daisy.

"Pssst," whispered the stranger in a
deep mysterious voice. "Have you seen
006 and a Bit anywhere?"

Daisy stared back at the stranger in surprise.
She put her dark glasses on again quickly
and sat up straight.

"Yes I have seen 006 and a Bit!" she nodded.
"That's me! I am 006 and a Bit!"

"That is good news," whispered the stranger,
"because my name is 0021 and a Bit.
I am a real spy too!"

"The coloured sprinkles will be meeting with the chocolate flake on the vanilla ice-cream at tea time," whispered 0021 and a Bit.

"And the crunchy cream biscuits and lemonade will be meeting under the big yellow duvet when the clock strikes twelve," continued the mysterious stranger.

006 and a Bit frowned for a moment and clapped her hands excitedly. "Ooh goody! I know what that means!

We're having my favourite pudding for tea and then a midnight feast in your bed tonight! I'll bring my comic and my torch too!"

Which, as anybody knows, means
"Thanks, Mum. You're the
best spy in the world!"